Dreams of Golf

by
Maia Wojciechowska

Illustration & Design
by
A.K. Karsky

Pebble Beach Press, Ltd.

First Edition

Library of Congress Catalog
Card No. 93-084729
ISBN #1-883740-01-0

Manufactured in the United States
of America

This book is dedicated to all children and adults who did not have enough time with their father — like, Jody, Maria, Mike, Mark, Maia, Jim and me. We trust that chain will now break.

C.R.W.

Chapter 1

His father named him Ben. He was the only boy named Ben that year in Japan. They lived in the fishing village of Shimizu on Suruga Bay in the shadow of Mount Fuji. When he was four; his father explained to him why he gave him that name.

"You are named after Ben Hogan, my greatest hero. He won both the U.S. Open and British Open in 1953, the year I was born. Only two other men, both Americans, ever did that before him. And I want you to remember their names: Bobby Jones and Gene Sarazen."

He waited for the boy to repeat those strange names and the boy did, saying them exactly as his father said them. And then the boy waited for his father to tell him more.

"I could have named you Bobby or Gene. But I thought it should be Ben. Because it was Ben Hogan, and not Bobby Jones or Gene Sarazen who won those two titles the very year I was born."

"I like my name," the boy said and smiled up at his father. He was not going to mind other children laughing at his name any more; he was going to be proud of it now.

At four he was too young to understand what those three Golfers meant to his father. At four he did not yet know that those three Americans meant a great deal to his father. All three were his father's heroes. His father shared with them a dream, a dream of golf. All the boy knew was that his father was giving up his fishing job to take up golf, "for a living." That's what everybody said, his mother and his grandparents and all their friends. His father was now going to play golf as a professional.

"Your father has wanted to be a professional golfer ever since I've known him," his mother told Ben. "He had that one, great, impossible dream: to be a professional golfer. And now, you see, he is one! And he is so happy!"

His father, after that was very rarely home. For years the boy would think that to turn professional was to run away from home. And the boy missed his father very much and did not know what he could do to have him back home with him.

"He started too late," the boy overheard his uncle say to his mother. "He should have started as a small child. Then he would have had a chance at being the best. But he was seventeen when he first picked up a golf club."

"It does not matter how late a dream comes true," his mother said to him. "My husband's dream had been my dream as well."

"He will never win any of the major tournaments because he is too old." That's what a man said on television one day and the boy thought the man a liar.

"Your father has the will to win," his mother told him once when he woke up from a nightmare, "you could will your nightmares away."

The boy's nightmares had to do with his father's dream. In his nightmares the boy was always looking for his father and never finding him.

The first time the boy saw his father win on television, his mother cried.

"Why are you crying!" he asked her, thinking that she should be happy instead.

"I am crying because now he will love golf more than anything else," his mother said.

"More than me?" the boy asked. His mother just put her arms around him. She cried a little while longer, but he did not cry although he felt like crying. He missed his father more than ever that day, the day that he saw his father win that first tournament.

Sometimes when the boy looked very sad his mother would talk to him about his father, and he loved it, hearing about him.

"Even when he was a little boy, not much bigger than you," she would say, "he wanted to play golf."

"Did you know him then?"

"No. But his mother told me stories about him when he was a child."

"Go on."

"Golf to him was everything. But he could not play it. There was no money for golf clubs. So he went to school and dreamed about golf. And later, when he was a little bit bigger he began to work in the cannery after school. To earn money for his golf clubs."

"How old was he when he got his first clubs?"

"He was seventeen."

"Did he play much then?"

"Not much, because he had to work. His father's fishing boat sank and he had to support the family. He gave up going to school and worked very hard, sometimes fifteen hours a day..."

"He had no time for golf?"

"When I met him he told me that he played eighteen holes a day, each and every day and then he laughed and said he played golf inside his head..."

"How could he do that?" the boy asked his mother.

"In his imagination," she said and he knew what she meant. He often imagined that his father was with him. He imagined playing with him, and he imagined his father teaching him how to do what he did so well, how to play golf.

"You know, the day we were married, your father asked me if I would be willing to work so that he could play professionally. And I said, of course... You see, Ben, I always shared your father's dream of golf."

"Why do people say he started so late?" the boy wanted to know, not accepting the fact that his father started later than most.

"He wanted to put away some money in the bank. For you. He wanted a son very much. And when you were born he didn't want me to work, so it took a little longer for him to get started. You know how life is..."

The boy was beginning to see how life was. And life was hard and not always what one dreamed about. But now he understood about his father. He understood that his father's dreams had to wait for a long time to happen. And he thought that his dream, of having a father around would also have to wait as well.

His mother loved to talk to him about his father as much as he loved to listen to her. He got to know his father from what she told him. And he liked very much what he heard, and what he liked especially was being told by his mother that he was "very much like his father." And now Ben had his own dreams. His dreams had to do with his father coming home, living with them, even for a little while.

"Can't he play here, in Japan, more often?" the boy wanted to know.

"He can't do both: be with us and follow his dream. To try to earn a living playing golf he has to travel. Most of the important tournaments are in America."

The boy often thought of America and wondered if his father liked it there. By the time Ben was five and a half his father wrote a letter telling Ben and his mother that he wanted them to move to the United States. There were two plane tickets inside the letter. His mother cried and he asked her why she was crying. He did not know if he should be sad or glad.

"Your father loves golf, but he loves us as well," his mother said hugging him hard. "In America he will see us more often. Maybe he will even live with us. And then my own dream will come true."

Chapter 2

The first night in America in his new house, Ben cried because his father was not there with them. The next night he cried because his grandmother was not there to say good night to him. The day after that he cried because his grandfather was not there to play with him. And for a whole week he cried because none of his friends were in America with him.

In time he stopped crying. In time he accepted America as the place where he was to live if he wanted to see his father at all. He saw him more often on television than he saw him in the flesh. On television they always talked about his father's age.

"Why do they always have to talk about his age?" his mother would ask the boy as if he could know the answer to the question. "Your father is not old! He is barely thirty four!"

The boy did not know what he could say to her. He didn't understand about being too old at thirty four or too young at six.

"You are too young for golf," his mother told him the first time she saw him swing one of his father's clubs. "You have to wait until you grow up a little. Your father will get you children's clubs one day. You wait and see."

But it was too hard to wait.

One day, while walking in the woods he found a golf club that was just his size. The shaft had broken in half and he put some tape around the broken part and now he could swing more easily with it than with his father's tall clubs. He got one of his father's golf balls and he kept hitting it on the lawn until he hit it too far and he lost it in the woods. But the same day he lost his ball, he found another. He found more than one; he found almost a dozen.

Ben and his mother lived next to a golf course in a little house where his father had hoped to spend a lot of time.

"It will be wonderful living here," he told them the first time he came home. "The golf club is next door and I might become a pro there, once I retire..."

That was a dream. Now he had to be on a tour and "make the cut." That was very important to him, although the boy did not understand what that meant. All the boy knew was that his father was a rare visitor in his own house.

"It is not easy being away from you two," Ben overheard his father tell his mother one night. "Sometimes I wonder if it is worth the price. But you see if one plays professional golf, one cannot do it once in a while; one has to be playing all the time. You get used to the pressure, you improve your game, you work hard. And sometimes you see the results, but often you begin to wonder, is it worth it? But each time that question arises I think to myself, I have such a short time, I came to it all so much later than others, and that is why I have to make the most of it. And you know, I love competition golf more than anything else in the world."

"More than Ben, more than me?" she asked.

"Of course not!" Ben's father said loudly, and then he lowered his voice so that Ben barely heard what he said next: "It's me against time. Maybe next year will be my last. I have to go on as long as I can. The end will come soon enough."

"Do you still love it, the game as much as you loved it at first?" his wife wanted to know.

"I love it more than life," he told her.

"Why do you love it so?" she asked.

"It's a game that takes a measure of an individual man. It's all up to you with little interference from others," he replied.

"And you always measure up?"

"Often enough I do, because I only have to depend on me."

The boy often thought of his father's words, but he did not understand their meaning. He only understood the fact that his father did what he had to do to measure up in his own eyes. He thought about this a lot and wondered when he, too, would have to measure up.

By the time he was seven Ben had a secret that even his mother didn't know anything about. He would wake up very early in the morning. He would climb out of his bedroom window an hour before his mother would wake and walk to the golf course. There were two holes, a par 3 and a par 4, that skirted around, close to his house, on which he would play alone for an hour. By watching the golfers, Ben had learned that nobody would be playing those holes that early in the morning. At that time even the early starters would not reach the fifteenth and the sixteenth holes. But sometimes the sprinklers would go on and Ben would come home soaking wet. He would hide his wet clothes under the bed so his mother would not see them, and he would not have to explain.

He only had that one club he found and an old putter that he had bought for a quarter at a garage sale. But he had plenty of balls because he would find them in the woods. And there was a field, not far from home, where he would hit the balls, for he hit them now too far to play on his own lawn.

His putter was a bit too tall for him, but he didn't mind because he would grip it down the shaft. He had learned his swing from watching his father on television. But putting was not as easy to learn from watching. Putting was something you had to do well if you were to be a golfer. Nobody told him that but he knew it, putting was like finishing something. To start was easy, but to finish was hard. And it was putting that he practiced on those two holes early in the morning. He loved those two greens. He overheard players say that those were the toughest greens on the course, and sometimes he heard men use bad swear words when they would miss a putt. The fifteenth green was the trickier of the two. The boy found out in time that it was wiser to hit below the pin and have an uphill putt. All the downhill putts on this green picked up speed, and when the pin was placed on the lowest portion, the ball would roll off the green unless it went into the hole. The boy loved this green because no two putts were ever the same. Each angle was different, uphill putts and downhill putts had variations of their own, and the breaks ranged from very slight to incredible.

The sixteenth green was very different. It had three layers and to play it well one had to consider how wet or dry the grass was, and when it was cut. Sometimes even the breeze seemed to make a difference on this green. The trick in playing this green was to land on the tier with the pin; otherwise one could not beat this green.

Sometimes he would wait to see early players come around to the sixteenth green. He loved to stand behind a tree and hear them talk about what he now considered as his own two greens. They always spoke badly about them, some with fear and some with hatred. And words like "crazy" and "stupid" and "impossible" were often used to describe what the boy was mastering now. He was a small kid but putting on those two greens made him equal to the best of the club's players. And knowing this made him very glad. He didn't understand those who feared or hated this green.

He wished he could take some lessons but didn't dare ask his mother, afraid that she would say no, that he was far too young to start.

By the time he was eight Ben decided that nobody was ever going to know about his golf. It was to be his own secret. One day Ben found a driver and a five iron. He found the clubs in his own back yard. Someone must have tossed them away in anger. He now had three clubs and then he bought himself a new putter. He started playing golf in earnest. He wished he could play golf all the time. Instead, he had to go to school, because the summer of his eighth year was over.

He did not like school at all. It was far too noisy for him. There were kids screaming and screeching and fighting and laughing and talking too loudly. None of them were his friends. He was "too polite" some said. He was "different," others thought, and one little boy said that Ben was, "not at all like us."

Ben went to school, but most of the time he was there, he imagined himself playing not only the two holes, but all eighteen holes of the golf course. Inside his head Ben was playing golf each and every school day. All through the day.

Chapter 3

For his ninth birthday his father gave him a book written by Ben Hogan. It was from that book, he would say years later, he learned how to play the game of golf.

Each day after school, Ben would take Hogan's book out to the back yard with him and would read from it and then practice what he learned. His mother was working at her typewriter and never interrupted. Sometimes, when he hit the whiffle ball just right, he had the feeling that a real ball would have made his father proud.

If it was not for golf, dreaming about playing it, wanting to play it, Ben would have been a very unhappy little boy.

His mother would often say, "You should have some friends over."

He had no friends. All the boys in his school were interested in baseball and football and basketball. Not one was interested in golf. Team sports were easier, they thought, you could depend on the others on the team. You could also be disappointed by them. Ben didn't want to depend on or be disappointed by anyone. And as he grew, he didn't know it but he was becoming an individual, a special person, different from anyone else. "But you are growing up so differently from Japanese boys," his mother said to him one day, "Why am I different? How am I different?" he wanted to know.

"You're becoming an individual."

He repeated that word and liked the sound of it.

"You're like nobody else in this whole world," his mother then said.

He discovered that he could play all eighteen holes at night. By the light of the moon. And that is what he did now, each time there was a full moon.

"Why do you look so tired?" his mother wanted to know.

He loved playing his solitary night games more than he loved anything else in his life. Unless he hit the ball straight down the fairway, with his five iron he could not find it, so he learned to hit the balls as straight as an arrow, and that pleased him a lot. And each night, it seemed to Ben, he would gain a few feet in length on his drives. When he started at the age of eight, he was hitting drives under one hundred yards, but in only a few months he was driving the ball fifty yards further.

On his tenth birthday his father gave Ben a set of clubs and told him that he would teach him how to play golf as soon as he got back from the PGA tour. But once the tour was over Ben's father had to go to Japan. By the time he actually found the time, Ben was already eleven and had played a lot of solitary golf, and his clubs were pretty much worn down.

He never played when others played. He only played before anyone was on the course, or at night, by the light of the moon. If anyone bothered to ask him why he played alone he would say that he was playing golf as an individual; he didn't want to depend on others.

But, Ben now had dreams of golf. He did not dream of being as good as the man he was named after. He did not dream of winning the British and U.S. Open. He no longer even dreamed of being taught golf by his father. Ben now had a new dream. He wanted to caddy for his father. He wanted to travel with him and carry his bag for him and he wanted more than anything to be near him, to see him playing the game which they both loved.

Ben dreamed about that, about being his father's caddy, both during the day and during the night. He dreamed about this all the time, when he rode in a school bus, in class and during lunch, and when he was doing his homework. He dreamed about it even when he watched television and ate his dinner and took his shower and lay down to go to sleep. The only time Ben did not dream about being his father's caddy was when he played golf himself. When he played golf Ben did not dream about anything. He only concentrated on hitting the ball. He concentrated on which club to use. He concentrated on his short game and most of all he concentrated on his putting. When Ben played golf, before anyone was on the golf course, or during the nights of full moon Ben did not dream his golf dream. He was working on getting better at his craft.

Chapter 4

When Ben was eleven his father came home for a whole week. The night he arrived he said to Ben,

"Tomorrow morning I will call the pro at the golf course and you will start your lessons. I would teach you golf myself except I don't believe that children learn best from their parents."

But tomorrow it rained. And it rained every day for the six days that his father was home.

"I spoke to the pro," Ben's father said before he left, "and he will give you a dozen lessons. And next time I come home we will play golf together. The pro, his son and you and I."

Ben did not like the pro. That was because of what the pro said to him the very first time he met him: "I don't think your father is as good as they say. I could be much better than he is, if I could afford to travel and leave my family behind. But I love my family so I teach golf and make a good living at it. If I went on the PGA tour I would win more money than your father does. But most of all, unlike your father, I would never have let Augusta get me!"

Ben wished the pro had not said anything at all about his father. He did not hit the balls well during his first lesson.

"You are small, like your father," the pro told him, "and small people have to compensate by really getting their bodies into it. Didn't your father teach you that? Didn't he teach you anything?"

Ben responded, "He taught me all I know," he said.

After saying that, he had to prove that he knew how to hit the ball. He hit the next dozen balls as well as he ever hit in his life and made the pro whistle in admiration.

"Hey, you are good! My son's been taking lessons from me for five years and he's a foot taller than you, but he can't hit the ball as far, nor as well."

"My father is a great teacher," said Ben and smiled to himself.

The pro said nothing, and then he reached into his pocket

and took out some money.

"Here, kid, take your dad's money. I can't teach you anything your father has not taught you already."

"You keep the money," said Ben to the pro. "It will be my bet, with you. If you ever play my father, my bet's on him to beat you."

After that Ben began to think about playing against others. But he didn't do it right away. He continued to play early in the morning and during the nights, but now he would work on his putting on the practice putting greens of the golf club. And when he reached the age of thirteen, he began to want to compete against others his age after school and on weekends, whenever he could.

They began to talk about him and his game. The older men and those who played the course for years began to say that he was going to be as good as his father.

"Look at his swing!"

"It's a classical swing, reminds me of Ben Hogan's swing."

"You've seen Ben Hogan play?"

"Sure did! Three times."

"You must be older than the hills."

"I am not as old as you might think. Didn't I beat you by five strokes last time we played?"

"The kid will be as good as his father..."

"He will be better..."

"Much better! His putting is great, and his dad's putting is what keeps him from the big money..."

Ben hated it, being compared to his father. There was nothing as silly, he thought, as being compared to him. Looking good and being good were two different things. He, unlike his father, had never been in a tournament. He had never played under pressure. His father was a pro, and he was just a kid, an amateur kid.

As Ben grew and got to be good at golf his dreams of golf did not change. Ben did not dream about playing with his father. He continued dreaming about caddying for his father. He dreamed about being with his father, talking to him, getting to know each other. He thought that he would miss him less and less as he grew older, but it was just the opposite. He missed his father more and more.

They heard about it on the television news. His picture appearing on the screen surprised Ben and his mother. They missed the first words of the news announcer.

"...the car accident happened in Spain where he was playing a PGA tournament; although not seriously hurt he is forced to cancel his European golf tour..."

Just then the phone rang; Ben answered it.

"I am now going to keep that promise," his father said. "I'll be coming home and together we will work on your golf game."

"Are you all right?" Ben asked. Hearing the television announcer he had been gripped by fear that his father might be seriously hurt, that he might never play again.

"I am fine, but my leg was cut a bit and the knee is stiff. I can't play for a while. I will be coming home."

After his mother had talked to Ben's father, there were tears of happiness in her eyes. She hugged her son to her and laughed. Ben had never seen her so happy.

"He's all right! And he will be home! He said for at least a few months! Do you know that we have seen him for no more than a few days in the past five years?"

He knew only too well. The longest time that his father had stayed with them occured six years ago, and that was for less than three weeks.

Chapter 5

When he came home he limped a bit and laughed about it.

"It's nothing! It's much better than it was, and it doesn't hurt as much."

"You don't know," Ben's mother said proudly, "but Ben has been playing golf. And everyone says he's very good."

"The lessons with the pro must have paid off."

"I love the game," the boy said to his father feeling nervous for the first time talking to him about golf. He had not dared to bring up the subject himself because of what he did with the money his father had given the pro.

"I'd like to play with you," his father said and smiled.

"What are you two waiting for?" Ben's mother said, and she shooed them out of the house.

It was a fine day and his father felt happy to be out with his clubs in the back of the car and his son beside him.

"How good is your game?" he wanted to know.

"You will have to judge for yourself," said Ben, a little scared now of what his father might think of his swing. It was faster and different from his father's, a more elongated swing.

Ben had hoped to avoid the pro, but he saw them right away and clapped his hands and laughed.

"Finally!" he said. "This must be my lucky day!" He reached out his hand to Ben's father and shook it, and with his other patted Ben on the head. Turning to Ben's father he said, "Your son made me a bet that you can take me on! We will see about that!"

Ben's father frowned at Ben, but Ben shook his head.

"Not today," Ben said to the pro. "I'd like to play with my father today. Just the two of us." This would be the very first time they could play together, and neither wanted that time to be spoiled.

"No way," said the pro. "I want to play him today. I'll be

taking off for vacation tomorrow, and God knows when I'll run into you again. Today's the day! You, Ben, can caddy for your dad, and I'll carry my own bag."

Ben knew that his father could not walk eighteen holes. He knew that his father's knee hurt him still. But he also knew that his father's sense of honor would not allow him to mention the fact that he was hurting, or out of practice, or that he wanted to take a cart. It was up to Ben to make those decisions. While the pro was getting his clubs, Ben got a cart. He put his own bags alongside his father's bag.

His father was smiling at him when he got in beside him. Ben was going to drive.

"Is it true you bet the pro that I can beat him?" he asked the boy.

"Of course," Ben said. "It was a very safe bet." And then he added, with sadness: "I won't get to play with you today."

"Why not? We could make a threesome," his father said.

"I know the pro. He's been wanting to take you on for a long time now. He's been talking about that for a long time... But are you up to playing him?"

His father looked at him for a moment and then nodded his head.

"Why the cart?" the pro asked coming out of his shop.

"We want to ride together today," said his father. "If you don't mind."

"It's all right with me," said the pro and got into another cart and led the way to the first tee.

"I never got around to playing this course," said Ben's father.

"The first hole is an easy par 5," Ben told his father, "with only a brook, in front of the green, to worry about and the sand traps on the right side. I think you can get on the green in two."

"I feel so out of practice," his father said. "I should have gone to the driving range first."

"Too late for that," said the pro who overheard the remark. He watched Ben's father get out of the cart and wince as his leg touched the ground. He had heard and read about the car accident. He was glad to have an advantage. He smiled as he was teeing up.

Ben wondered if his father's doctors would have approved of him playing so soon. And then Ben heard the pro's driver hit the ball.

The pro's shot went to the right, but lay safe some 235 yards away. The pro walked to his cart, sat down and looked at Ben's father take a practice swing. To the boy the swing looked great, but to his father it did not feel right. He took another practice swing. And still another.

Ben had spotted two deer and was looking at them when he heard the twang of wood on the club but missed seeing his father's drive. And now he was afraid that his father, having not practiced for so long, had hit a bad shot.

"Where did it go?" he asked after his father got into the cart. "I didn't see it."

His father pointed straight ahead.

The ball lay some three hundred yards, straight down the middle. The boy smiled at his father and Ben's father smiled back at him.

On his second shot the pro missed making the green and went into the brook. He two putted and came out with a bogey, while Ben's father putted for and made an eagle.

He had often imagined his father playing the course, and he had always thought that he would eagle the first hole.

"Have to make up three," said the pro as he shot his cart ahead of them to the next tee.

"What club do you play here?" his father asked as they approached the second hole, a par 3.

"I used to play a seven, but now I always play an eight," said Ben pleased to be asked. His father gave him a surprised look.

"How long have you been playing?"

"For a while now, as often as I can; it's never often enough,"

Ben replied and his father smiled at him. His father took a nine out of his bag.

"Easy hole," said the pro not giving Ben's father's honors but teeing up his ball. He hit it well. It made a perfect arc over the right bunker and rolled on the green, within two feet of the hole. "Easy hole" the pro repeated and then laughed.

Ben's father's easy swing reminded Ben of the time a TV commentator described it as "the swing that goes at the ball like a knife through butter." The ball rose higher than it should, Ben thought, and landed past the hole, then spun backwards and came to rest within a few inches of it. "Easy hole," said Ben to the pro. As they drove towards the green Ben asked his father how he felt.

"I feel all right," his father told him, "but I don't think I will be able to finish. Will you take over for me if I can't? It will be for the bet you made."

"Of course," said Ben and once again he felt the wave of happiness and pride at his father's trust.

Both men made birdies and went to the third hole. "You are still three ahead but I'll be catching up," said the pro and once again he laughed.

"I don't like him," said Ben in a whisper, but his father might not have heard. He was looking toward the green, some 460 yards away.

"What do I watch out for?" asked Ben's father.

"Stay out of the right side. That bunker's about 250 yards. If you go into the woods, it's a *sayonara* ball because there is a stream that eats up the stray balls. Three bunkers guarding the green are tough; the deepest is in the center. But it's the green, the worse green until you come to the 15th and 16th. On this one you've got to be downhill of the pin or you'll roll like mad."

"You'd make a good caddy," said his father and smiled at his son. "Next tournament, will you caddy for me, okay?"

Ben swallowed hard and smiled back at his father. Then he nodded his head afraid that his voice would betray his emotions. After all, the longest dream he ever had was coming true. He would caddy for his father!

The pro's shot went into the woods on the right, but so did Ben's father's.

Although they had Ben to help them look, neither player could find his ball, and they made their drop alongside of each other. They both were playing their third shot and both made it safely to the green. The placement of the pin, Ben told his father, was the easiest of the placements. But his father's putt came an inch short of the hole while the pro made his putt.

"Only two to make up," the pro said gunning his golf cart ahead of them.

"How many lessons did you take from him?" the father asked his son.

"One," Ben said. "He is a jerk," he added.

"You are becoming an American," his father said. Ben knew he would never have called any adult a jerk if they were still living in Japan.

Ben's father lost his two-stroke advantage on the seventh with another missed putt, and still another one eluded him on the eighth. The two men were tied coming off the ninth.

"Do you want to go on?" Ben asked his father.

"What do you mean, does he want to go on?" the pro laughed. "Of course we are going on!"

"I really don't like this man," his father whispered to Ben.

"But how do you feel?" Ben whispered back. He was very worried now about his father because his father did not look at all well.

"I am all right," his father said.

But he wasn't. It was easy to see. He had been in constant pain for some time. His instincts were guiding him while his will kept the pain at bay. When they came to the fourteenth hole, the score was still a tie. Ben's father turned to the pro.

"The wager is still on," he said, "but I'd like my son to take over now."

"Are you kidding?" said the pro.

Ben's father smiled, shook his head and said he wasn't kidding at all. He would like his son to finish the wager for him.

"O.K. It's your dough," said the pro.

Chapter 6

The pro hit his longest drive off the tee, straight down the fairway 310 yards.

Ben felt stiff; he should have stretched but there was no time now. The pro was watching him take a practice swing.

The boy hit a straight drive. It was much shorter than his best drives, slightly under 210 yards.

"That's the difference. A hundred yards and a hundred bucks," said the pro and laughed. He drove away, making a show of looking for lost balls as Ben attended to his second shot. He hit it further than his drive but he did not make the green; the ball stopped in the tall grass, the fringe of the green. The pro hit his beyond the green and ended lying behind a tree. Both Ben and his father saw as he kicked the ball into a clearer path to the flag but neither said anything at all. Except now they both knew that it was only their honor at stake; the pro had none.

Ben chipped, and the ball rolled right into the middle of the cup, for a birdie. His father gave a whistle of approval while the pro said nothing. He had chipped two feet from the hole and called it a "gimme." Then, he picked up the ball.

"One ahead for the kid," said the pro.

"Two ahead for me," thought the boy. "Maybe even three. He could easily have missed that putt."

"How is your putting?" asked Ben's father of his son. "Will I ever get a chance to see it, or do you always chip your balls into the cup?"

The boy smiled while his father laughed. He looked better now, some color had come back to his face.

"So, how is your putting?" he asked again.

"I don't have too much trouble putting," said Ben.

His father looked at him in admiration.

"That's always been the toughest part for me. I'm a notoriously bad putter."

"I've heard it said," Ben said to his father, "that nobody could beat you at this game but for your putting, which is very good but not great."

His father gave him a smile and now Ben asked him something he had meant to ask him since the tee.

"What was wrong with that lousy drive of mine?" Ben wanted to know.

"You didn't hit it full, like you hit the second shot," his father said.

"Will you teach me how to hit it the way you hit your drives?" Ben now asked his father.

"If you teach me how to putt," his father said and both smiled at each other.

"Watch me on the next two greens," said Ben. "They are notorious around here."

"Even I've heard about the 15th and the 16th green," said his father. "The real estate man, who sold me our house talked about them. How come you don't have trouble with them?"

"When I was a kid and the moon was out I used to sneak on them and practice with a putter I bought for a quarter at a garage sale."

"I wish I had been around you then," said his father.

On the fifteenth tee Ben closed his eyes and tried to see how his father hit his drives, the perfect arc, the shift of weight happening a split second before the impact of the club and ball. He held the mental picture of his father's drive when he swung, and his drive went further than the pro's.

They both were on the green in two. Ben smiled at his father as the pro putted, and smiled at him again before he made the putt.

"What the hell is going on here?" the pro asked, after Ben putted, while he himself took two to sink his, and considered himself lucky. "You are three ahead; I'm three behind."

"Actually four," Ben thought inside his head. "Maybe even five."

The boy hit a drive that went further than the pro's on the 17th. And the pro was in no mood to talk while pocketing his ball, having once again two putted while Ben's single putt found the hole.

"Four ahead, actually, five or perhaps even six," said his father and smiled. "There are no gimme's when you play for money or in a tournament, and the pro should know that."

He felt suddenly great. He had seen admiration in his father's eyes. He knew he was playing way above his head, but he should not have thought that because on the eighteenth tee he topped his ball. He had not done this in years. "I must be getting cocky," he said to himself as he approached the drive that barely went seventy yards while the pro's ball lay very far down the fairway. He topped the ball once again on his second shot.

"What am I doing?" he asked his father, feeling terribly ashamed and stupid about what he had done.

"I don't have to tell you, do I?" his father said.

"I looked up."

"That too. But you lost your concentration, didn't you?"

"I guess," the boy said.

His third shot was clean and came to rest eight feet from the pin. He finished the hole with only a bogey while the pro had a birdie on the last hole.

He feared it would be far worse. It was a scary finish but they had won!

"I got cocky," he said to his father.

"Yes, that costs tournaments, sometimes," his father said. "But you've won all the same."

"We have won, but I wish I could replay this last hole. I'd play it well, I know," said his son.

"Champions always think that way," said his father. "And you know what, I think you'll be a champion one day. I'd like to be your coach, starting now." The pro's cart almost bumped into theirs. His hand was extended towards Ben.

"Here is your money," said the pro, "and the extra ten is so you don't talk about it."

"You take it," said Ben handing him back the ten dollar bill, "I would have nothing to say. I didn't do so well."

The pro pocketed the bill.

"I'd like to play you alone one day," said the pro to Ben's father. "And as far as you are concerned, kid, you played way over your head."

"The man lacks grace," said his father watching the pro drive away. "You know, golf is the only game in the world where one needs grace to play well."

Ben thought that the comment most often applied to his father had been that he always played in "the state of grace." He had never quite understood what it had meant, and now he asked his father.

"What does it mean, to be in the state of grace?"

"One with God," his father said.

They were silent for a while, each thinking his own thoughts. When they got home, his father said what Ben had been waiting to hear for years:

"I am going to play the Masters. Will you caddy for me?"

"Will you caddy for me, Ben?" his father repeated.

Ben had tears in his eyes and he pretended to rub them as he said to his father that he would. He did not tell him how long he had waited for that dream to come true.

Chapter 7

"This is the beginning of October and we have five months to get ready."

Ben now smiled at his father and said, "Ben Hogan, after his car accident, took longer to get ready for the U.S. Open, sixteen months."

"Ben, I'm serious. I want you to help me to get ready for the Masters."

"How can I do that?"

"Every day, from now on, I want you to say to me: I know you can do it."

"I know you can do it!"

"Thank you. And there is something else."

"Anything!"

"I am going to concentrate on my putting at first. I want you to become my putting coach."

Again Ben's eyes filled with tears, but now he did not hide them. There were tears in his father's eyes as well.

"Let's start right now," said his father.

He got out his putter and a ball. He placed a dime on the smooth carpet about four feet from the ball. And then with his putter he stroked the ball. It went in a straight line but did not reach the dime. It came two inches short.

"What did I do wrong?" he asked his son.

"Your left wrist was not firm enough," said Ben. "There should be no motion in a wrist."

"My left wrist always breaks slightly during the stroke," his father said.

"If you are not happy with your putting you have to change that. Make your wrist firm."

"I've never done it with a firm wrist."

Ben placed his hand over his father's wrist and held it as his father made a practice putt. Then he placed the ball five feet from the dime.

"Hit it with it firm," he ordered his father.

His father did as he was told and the ball went straight at the dime and stopped right behind it.

"Good," said Ben.

"The power of positive putting," said his father and smiled.

And that's how the training began. Every day now, while Ben was in school, his father worked on his putting, on the stroke that was new to him and that he now adopted as his own. And every day after Ben came back from school, he told his father, "I know you can do it."

They both knew what it meant. What he had to do was to overcome his greatest fear. And that was the fear that he could not conquer Augusta, the course on which the Masters is played.

Now the real work began. Each day he would talk to Ben and tell him what he intended to do now that he was living up to his promise to conquer Augusta.

"For me it's the entire course. I have to conquer the entire course. From the first tee to the last hole. The others will mostly worry about those tree holes of the Amen Corner. You see, Ben, I was defeated by all of it. And besides, the Amen Corner comes on the back nine. When I played there I got defeated at the very start. What I intend to do is master Augusta. Because last time Augusta mastered me. I have to conquer it because I've never recovered from that defeat. And I have to recover from it now."

"But how will you do it, how will you conquer Augusta?" Ben wanted to know.

The first time he asked that question his father said, "With God's help." The second time he asked it, his father said, "With my will and determination."

The third time he asked the question, his father said, "With your help. My caddy's help." And that's when Ben's part in conquering Augusta began.

Everything was different now with Ben's life. Having his

father waiting for him to come home from school made him happy. And being happy changed everything! The way he looked, the way he felt and the way he thought.

He always felt that there was no one who liked him at his school. He thought he had no friends at all. And yet, one day, in the early fall of the year his father came home, Ben was elected school president! That same day, he was surprised to read in his school paper that he was "... the student most admired for his academic achievements, his thoughtfulness and politeness. Ben is considered, by both teachers and students to have the brightest future. Everyone agrees that he will succeed in his desire to follow in his father's footsteps and become a great golfer."

Ben never had any trouble with his studies, but he had never really been all that interested in anything he was learning in school. He just did his work. He felt no pleasure in having the best grades in his class. He was sure that he would forget what he learned the day after the tests were over. But now, suddenly, everything he was studying interested him. The textbooks, which each year seemed duller, miraculously became fascinating to him. He discovered, with joy, that he developed a great hunger for knowledge.

What surprised Ben most of all was that he could manage, with ease, and equally delight in, his two lives: his life as a schoolboy and his life of golf.

Suddenly everything had its time and its place; it seemed to Ben that there was an order to God's universe. He realized that the family, being physically together and together in its dreams, was what made all the difference in the world.

"I've never been so happy," his mother said to him one day.

"I've never been so happy," he said to her in reply.

"I've never been so happy," his father said to them both one night at the beginning of March.

Chapter 8

It started two weeks before the Masters. The first to come were newspaper people from Japan, followed by television crews from Japan. They were joined by others, from all over the world, so many others that Ben's mother called it "the media locusts".

Their street, their back and front yards, their home, their very lives and everyday activities were now invaded by those who wanted to interview Ben's father, photograph him, his family and talk to them. They had come to cover the story of "what could well become the greatest comeback story of all time," as one of them told his viewers.

Among the many who came, there was a young boy, not much older than Ben, who worked for a radio station in Japan that provided all sorts of sport information for students. He asked Ben for an interview, and Ben was pleased that they were going to speak Japanese and that the boy wanted to talk to him, rather than to his father.

"Why is that particular place, Augusta, so special?" he asked.

"It's very special to my father because it's the most important tournament in the world."

"I understand you will be your father's caddy there?"

"Yes," Ben said. He flushed with pleasure at the thought of it.

"Do you know it? Have you been there?"

"No. But I know about it. I've read a lot about Augusta. And my father and I have studied the course, hole by hole. We know each hazard..."

"Could you first tell us about Augusta, the story of the place..."

Ben shared what he had learned about Augusta from his father and from the articles and books he had read. There was no way to talk about Augusta without talking about Bobby Jones.

"One of the great legends of golf," the interviewer explained to his listeners.

"It was 1930," Ben told him, "Jones had won thirteen national titles, including the grand slam of golf. And then, at twenty eight, he decided to retire."

"Why? He had so many more years to play. He was on top of his game..."

"Maybe he grew tired of it. Or maybe, being on top he did not want to..."

His interviewer indicated that the tape had come to the end and while he inserted a new one into his recorder Ben thought about what his father said to him just the other day. "If I win the Masters I will retire. I want to have time for you. And your mother. I want to be around you, Ben. I want to give you the early start at golf that I never had. I want to teach you what I've learned."

"Why would Jones give up golf at such an early age when he was doing so well?" The interviewer repeated the question. "Did Bobby Jones give up playing competition golf because he wanted to do something else?"

"He had always wanted to design a dream golf course."

"How did he pick Augusta, in Georgia?"

"He had married a girl from there and he knew a man called Clifford Roberts. And Mr. Roberts had an interest in buying and selling things and he knew a famous nursery in Augusta called Fruitlands. It was a large parcel of land with many fruit and flowering trees like magnolias, dogwoods, azaleas... The setting seemed perfect to Jones for his dream course. It had gently rolling hills which reminded him of the British seaside courses which he loved very much. But what made it so incredibly beautiful, so like a dream, were all the flowers and the trees. In the spring, especially in April, everything is blazing with color."

"But to build a golf course wouldn't he have to destroy all that?"

"Oh, no! That is exactly what is so very special about Augusta. Jones was going to keep the beauty of the place and work the course around it... Augusta had been described by many as 'the most beautiful 365 acres in the world,'" said Ben. "He teamed up with a retired Scottish doctor, Alister MacKenzie.

Maybe if they had known more about how to build a golf course they might have ruined that beautiful property. But they were never tempted to do that. They wanted to make those acres even more beautiful! You see, both men were in love with golf and believed that golf courses were meant to be beautiful."

Ben had watched with his father, hour after hour, day after day, video tapes of different golfers playing Augusta. One day he asked his father if the beauty of the place had distracted him when he played there. His father thought for a while and then said, "You know, Ben, maybe that is why it all went wrong for me. That whole day, that first day I played Augusta, might not have been such a disaster had I taken the time to smell the flowers! I never noticed how beautiful Augusta was! I never saw all those marvelous flowers, all those magnificent trees! All I saw, that day, was my ball. And most of the time it was where it shouldn't have been."

He stopped for a moment, and in the silence of the room Ben heard the echo of his father's regret. He saw sorrow on his face.

"Sometimes," his father said now, "we think that we have to concentrate so much, work so hard, that it all escapes us! The sense of the beauty escapes us, the essence of life. Maybe it's more so with us, the Japanese, than with any other people. Or maybe it's like that with anyone who is not in tune with the eternal... You see, Ben, when I played Augusta, I played as if there was no God."

"It will be different this time," Ben said to his father.

"That time I played the Masters, I was all caught up in the present, in the moment. I never felt that there was yesterday, that there will be a tomorrow, that God exists across space. I never thought of you, or your mother, nor prayed to God, nor gave thanks for being where I was. I never saw anything at all. To be able to win, at anything, I've learned since, you cannot shut out life. And that is what I did that day, shut out everything except for the desire to win. And you know what, Ben, I no longer think I got conquered by Augusta. I think I defeated myself!"

And then he laughed. And Ben laughed with him, although he did not understand as much as his father seemed to have understood. Yet something about his father told him that he was far wiser now then he had ever been. Ben knew now, that whether his father won or lost the Masters, he would be playing his best there.

There were times Ben hated all the interviews his father had to give, and other times he loved listening to them, most especially to those news people who asked the kind of questions that interested him.

"From all you've learned, how does Augusta differ and how is it similar to other great courses?"

His father smiled, also liking the question.

"Augusta National," he answered, "like all the other great courses, such as St. Andrew's and Winged Foot and Merion and Oakmont and Pebble Beach, is really a thinking man's golf course. But you've got to figure Augusta out from the green back to the tee, because it's not an obvious course. It's subtle, like a dream. Other courses you can play from the tee toward the green, but it is not like that with Augusta."

"What about the greens in Augusta?"

"Oh, they're fast! Three putts are common, because balls bounce and roll across yards of the greens. And the angles, the angles from which you approach those greens, are most important!

"Have you studied those greens from an armchair?"

"Sitting in an armchair watching films, miles and miles of video clips! With my putting coach, my son. That part, the armchair part, is theory, you might say, and educated guesses and scientific research. And then there is practice. I've been practicing putting, which had always been my weakness..."

"How can your son be your putting coach? Isn't it true that he's never played a tournament?"

"He's a believer that my putting can be as great as his is already. When he starts playing tournament, you will see for yourself what a natural player and what an expert putter he is. He's a good teacher, maybe only because he's a good learner?"

There were miles of words written about Augusta that year, and many who thought they knew all about it learned a few facts they did not know. And those who knew nothing about it found they wanted to learn more.

"Can a golf course capture the imagination of a nation?" asked a Japanese writer that early spring. "Augusta is all one hears about. Is it really that tough a course? Since 1934 there is not a single hole at Augusta National Golf Club that had not been eagled! Two of its par-fives have been scored in two! Three of its par-threes have been holed in one! The lowest score at Augusta has been registered as a fabulous 35, thirty-seven strokes below par!

"But there have been many more disasters than triumphs there. One professional golfer, back in 1935 needed twelve strokes to finish the 8th, a par-five. Another pro, in 1950 had an eleven on the 16th, a par-three. The following year another man who made his money off golf took a twelve on the 12th hole, another par-three. And that same year the great Sam Snead having shot a 68 the day before, finished with an 80 the following day.

"But no single pro had been so humbled by Augusta as our player from Japan. Will his own son, who will caddy for him in a few days, see him redeemed? Or will the son see his father, once again, humbled by it? Like no other tournament the Masters never fails to provide drama and suspense. This year our country will breathlessly watch one of her own try to wrestle with a golf course that so often defeats the very best among golfers."

Chapter 9

The first time Ben saw Augusta National Golf Club it was from the air. The plane's pilot made the announcement, "If you look on the right side of the plane you will be able to see the famed golf course where the Masters is played. One of our passengers today will be competing there in a few days. And the whole crew wishes him the best of luck."

To Ben, from the air the course looked like a giant winged green creature. He recognized the Amen Corner, that most awesome double triangle, with Rae's Creek, like a wide double edged knife, cutting into the twelfth hole. From up above, that green giant seemed waiting. Could his father conquer it, Ben wondered. Their combat would be waged in the clearings, the strips of lighter green flanked on both sides by what seemed like a dark jungle. And then, as suddenly as it appeared, the green giant vanished. Ben could see it no longer.

"What did it look like to you?" his father wanted to know.

"It looked so different, from what I thought it would," was all that Ben could say. He felt frightened.

"It looked like an angel flying with its wings spread out," his father said.

Ben sighed with relief. His father was not afraid of the monster after all. He saw it as an angel.

"You know, Ben," his father now said smiling at his son, "that one time I played Augusta I saw it all through fear. It looked like - it felt like some monster to me! Funny, isn't it, the prettiest golf course in the world looking like a monster! Fear does strange things to us!"

Ben wondered if perhaps his father had read his mind, knew his thoughts, had guessed how he saw Augusta. He had been scared, all along, from the moment his father asked him to caddy for him. He had been afraid that he would see his father lose. Suddenly he felt very ashamed of his lack of faith in him.

"Augusta," his father now said, "is not like any other golf

course in the world. I've read somewhere that it's the closest to being an open air cathedral. It's a work of God as much as it is a work of Man. The design of the course is Bobby Jones', but all those trees, all those flowers, all that beauty is God's. But when I went there I knew nothing of this. I should have been amazed, delighted, grateful just to be there. But instead I withdrew into myself. And inside myself I found fear. And fear made me blind to everything else."

He stopped speaking for a moment and looked at his son, and then he put his hand over his son's hand.

"I don't know how to explain it to you, Ben, but fear is something you don't want to keep company with. It's dangerous. It's ugly, and it is a destroyer. I gave in completely to fear that day in Augusta. And after it was all over, after I had played so badly, lost so shamefully, I thought that I could never play there again."

"But this time you will win!"

His father smiled.

"I don't know about that, but this time instead of fear I'll enjoy myself, and that's because I have you as my caddy!"

The second time Ben saw Augusta National Golf Club was by moonlight. His father had taken him to walk the course, their first night there. The air was sweet with the smell of flowers in bloom. Trees cast shadows on the grass. And the fairways did not look like combat zones to Ben. They looked great. It was almost light enough for them to play, but they did not come here to do that. They came here to, as father said, "walk it tonight in awe and admiration."

"It is so beautiful," the boy said and sighed.

"Yes, isn't it? Incredibly beautiful." His father spoke in a gentle voice. So much love went into making this wonder of a place."

An owl hooted somewhere and the squeak of a night animal followed the hoot. In the moonlight Ben noticed how soft his father's face looked.

"You know, Ben, the great thing about life is that you learn from your mistakes. You know, you sjmply can't repeat past mistakes. You might make new ones, but you certainly can't make the same mistakes twice."

They walked past the deep bunkers guarding the second green in silence, Ben wishing his father would tell him more about life. But his father was silent for a while. It was not until they turned and faced the dog leg of the fifth hole his father spoke again.

"How very privileged this place is! You know, Ben, this course was devised for a very few, for the very few men who can afford to take time to pleasure in life. Most of us live with our eyes fixed just ahead, we can't afford to look about. And we miss so very much... There is such generosity and such a gentleness to this place! It's a place not created for mere survival. It's a sort of place where we should come, when we grow tired of worrying about surviving, when we realize that there is more to life than struggle and strife. It's a marvel of a place! We are blessed just to be here."

They were suddenly overwhelmed by the sweet smell of azaleas brought to them by the gentle breeze from the west. And it was then that Ben became aware of the fact that he would remember this night for as long as he would live. And he wanted now to savor it all, remember every detail, every word, for this indeed was a very special place and a very special time, for both of them a shared moment in eternity.

"It's funny, Ben," his father said as they looked down the straight fairway of the 7th hole toward its five bunkers surrounding the green, "I never was simply grateful to be here when I first came. I just wanted to win. I wasn't ready to play it because I couldn't enjoy the moment. The course did not play for me. Everything became awkward, wrong, fearful! I wanted to make this place serve me. And this place is a miracle. And miracles don't serve anyone but God. Funny that I should once have feared a miracle!"

"What should you do with miracles?" the boy asked.

"I think you should, first of all be grateful for them. And then, I think you should thank God for letting you see them."

Ben thought that his father was speaking not only of Augusta, but of the many miracles of life. And suddenly he began to love it all! His father being well, his dream of caddying for him coming true! Being with him here in Augusta! And now the beauty of the course began to etch itself in his consciousness. He suddenly saw it differently. Everything began to make sense to him: the respect for the land, the way the hazards were placed, the angles to the land, and the care that went into creating the course. It all now belonged in the scheme of things, in the eternal logic, inside the order of the entire universe! And it was then that Ben knew that he was here to do a job, for his father as much as for himself, the job had to do with learning for both of them.

"What do you think will be the hardest thing for you here in Augusta, this time?"

"The hardest of all will be finding that delicate balance, between not being too distracted and yet being able to enjoy it all, the course, the other players and the crowd. I don't want to make the mistake I made that first time here. I don't want to sacrifice everything so that I would simply concentrate on playing. I don't think you can win that way. And I do want to win; at the same time I want to pleasure in the moment."

Ben had admired his father all his life. But now he found himself admiring him for the risk he was taking, the change he was willing to make. He knew it took courage, to do this, and he now admired his father's courage.

"The world is full of miracles," the television commentator said looking directly at the camera. "The one player known for his absolute concentration, never looking at anything else but his own ball, told me today that to win at golf, as in life, you have to appreciate everything around you and make the best of it."

Just before they started off; his father put his hand on Ben's shoulder and, looking directly at him, said;

"Ben, we worked hard and long to get here. Now it is our turn to fulfill that dream of ours. Let's enjoy every moment and thank God for this opportunity!"

He then smiled at his son and looked around at the very small crowd that was going to follow them. He had been teamed up with two players who were new to the game of tournament play. Ben heard his father wish them luck, then he stepped to the tee, took the driver Ben handed him and as a reporter would write that night:

"... he began to make history from the very first tee. The most incredible thing of all was the fact that his comeback was so totally different from what his fans expected. He seemed now a different man. He smiled often. He even laughed with his son. And he took time to smell the flowers... And as he came to the 18th green, that last day, leading the field by five strokes, he walked up to his son and lifted up his hand. He continued to walk with his son's hand held up in the air as the crowd kept roaring and applauding. And his son, Ben, who had caddied for his father, had tears in his eyes as their shared dreams of golf became reality."

EXPLANATION OF SOME "GOLF TERMS" COMMONLY USED

AUGUSTA - The famous golf course in the State of Georgia, where the "Masters" tournament is played each year in the month of April. The Masters is considered a very important tournament. It is often referred to as one of the "major" golf tournaments on the professional golf tour.

CADDY - A person carrying the golf clubs in a "Bag" for a player. A caddy is very important, as he/she advises the player on which club to use, where to hit the ball, and how to putt on the green, to get the ball in the hole the fewest number of times.

GOLF COURSE - The terrain that the game of golf is played on. It can be a nine hole golf course, most often it is an eighteen hole golf course.

GOLF HOLE - The part of a golf course where play starts on a "Tee" and ends on a "Green"

TEE - The starting part of each golf hole. Also, a wooden peg to place into the ground, upon which a golf ball rests in an elevated position so that it may be hit with ease. The wooden tee is only allowed on the starting tee of every golf hole.

GREEN - The ending part on each golf hole, a smooth surface of grass where the cup is placed.

CUP - A hole in the surface of the green, into which the golfer tries to hit the ball in the fewest number of strokes.

STROKE(S) - The number of times a golfer hits, or strikes the ball in an effort to get the ball into the hole.

GOLF BALL - A hard, white, yellow or red ball approximately 1 3/4 inches in diameter, whose surface is covered with small dimples.

GOLF CLUB - The place where golf courses are, a private or public place. Also, golf clubs are the "sticks" with heads on one end of the shaft and grips on the opposite end. These sticks are held by the grip with both hands and the ball is hit with the head of the golf club. There are three basic kinds of golf clubs; the "Woods", the "Irons", and the "Putter". The woods are used for long hits, the irons for shorter hits, and the putter is used on the green.

DRIVER -　The golf club used from the tee to hit the ball as far as possible. It is considered a wood, even though it is sometimes made out of metal.

PUTTER -　A flat faced golf club used on the greens to roll the ball into the hole.

PITCHING WEDGE -　An iron club used for short lofted hits to the green. A sand wedge is similar; it is used to hit from sand traps.

GOLF SCORE -　The object is to get the lowest score. On each hole every golfer counts the strokes (the times that he/she hits the ball until it goes into the hole). The total number of hits is added on each hole, and then the total number of hits or strokes is added for the nine holes and the eighteen holes; that total number is the golfer's score.

PAR -　A number, indicating the number of hits a golfer should have from the tee to the cup, based on the length of each hole. When added together for all the holes on the golf course, "Par" is the number of hits on the entire golf course. Each hole can be a par 3, par 4, or a par 5. A par 3 hole is the shortest, par 4 is longer, and the par 5 holes are the longest. Usually for each nine holes of a golf course there are two par 3 holes, five par 4 holes, and two par 5 holes, adding up to par 36 for each nine holes, or par 72 for each eighteen hole golf course. The score is often referred to in the term of par. As an example, if a golfer hits the ball three times on a par 3 hole, the golfer has "made par".

BIRDIE -　The score on any golf hole which is one less than par.

BOGEY -　The score on any golf hole which is one more than par.

EAGLE -　The score on any golf hole which is two strokes less than par. (an extremely good score)

FAIRWAY -　To make a good score, golfers aim for the fairway when they hit from the tee. That part of the golf course which is between the tee and the green, on most holes. The grass is mowed short on the fairway as opposed to the "rough" where the grass is left to grow higher on purpose, so that if a golfer misses the fairway, it will be more difficult to hit the ball from the rough.

BUNKER - An area on each golf hole where sand is placed, also called a "Sand Trap". These areas are difficult to hit from. Some bunkers or sand traps are located on the fairways, but most of the time they are located around the greens. The bunker is placed so that a golfer who hits the ball incorrectly is penalized by having to hit from the sand (also sometimes referred to as the beach).

HAZARDS - Areas on the golf course that are difficult and some times impossible to hit from, such as lakes, streams, woods and ravines. Bunkers are also considered hazards.

PENALTY STROKES - A lost ball or one hit into a hazard causes a golfer to be penalized by adding a stroke to the golfer's score. Certain penalties call for "Stroke and Distance", this penalty means the golfer must not only add a stroke to his/her score, but must also go back and try again from where he/she first hit the ball.

FLAG - A flag is placed inside the cup of every hole on the greens. Golfers use the height of the flag to judge the distance from the hole. The flag is removed from the cup once the ball is on the green, before the golfer putts the ball into the hole.

YARDAGE - The measurement of the length of each hole. Distance from the tee to the green. All distances on a golf course are usually measured in yards instead of feet.

PRO TOUR - The professional golfers move from golf course to golf course located in different cities. Every week they "tour" the country and sometimes they go to foreign countries to play on the "tour". This series of golf events throughout the calendar year is the "Pro Tour".

WHIFFLE BALL - A practice ball made of plastic. It is hollow and has holes in it. When hit, it does not go far. It is used by golfers in their back yards at home where the distance to hit a regular golf ball is limited. The whiffle ball will not break glass or cause damage such as that from a regular golf ball.

GIMME - A term used when a player allows another player to pick up the ball and not putt it into the hole, usually because it is so close and to save time. In tournaments and when bets are made, no "gimme's" are ever allowed.

Publisher's Acknowledgements:

Without these wonderful people, this book could not have happened. We thank each and everyone for their support, confidence and guidance. Especially Dick Laws of Truepenny Books, Inc. Tuscon, Arizona - he got the "big ball" rolling and keeps it from tumbling off the path which is paved with excellent book making. What a coach!

The author gets a special thanks. It's been a while since she won the Newberry Award for "Shadow Of A Bull". Now she is back where she belongs. John Strednansky did an excellent job of typesetting. Thanks, John. Mary Drag, a lifelong friend and the best teacher/editor. Thanks, Mary. Les Henkel, whose knowledge made it so we all can afford this book. Thanks, Les.

Without saying, Angela inspired A. K. Karsky and Pebble Beach Press, Ltd. to make it all happen, otherwise it would not.